Cinder

A Cinderella Tooting Tale

By John Mashni • Art by Kate Cosgrove

For Maxwell, Ella, Esme, and Temma
Who heard this story
a hundred times
before anyone else,
and who begged me to share it with you

CinderToot: A Cinderella Tooting Tale
By John Mashni

www.CinderToot.com
(check out the free stuff!)
www.JohnMashni.com
(secrets hidden here... look for clues)

Illustrated by Kate Cosgrove
Book design by Alissa DeGregorio

ISBN 978-1-7360706-0-4 (paperback)
ISBN 978-1-7360706-1-1 (ebook)

— THE —
INTENSE LIFE
PRESS

Published by The Intense Life Press, an imprint of The Intense Life LLC

This book is a work of fiction. Any similarity to actual events would be awesome. Though we have tried diligently to replicate the events in this book, none of us have had any success, especially in creating the prince's concoction and reproducing any of the smells of the maidens. And yes, I do want to make a scratch and sniff version. But I need to sell some copies of this version first.

The giant clock struck *once . . . twice . . . a third time.*

Cinderella gasped. Her fairy godmother had warned her to leave the ball before the clock struck twelve times, but Ella had been having too much fun with the prince to notice the hour.

The clock rang again. Jumping up, Ella raced toward the front doors of the palace. The prince chased after her. "Wait!" he cried. "I don't even know your name!"

Ella jumped down the palace's marble steps so quickly that one of her beautiful slippers fell from her foot. As she bent to pick it up, something happened. Something terrible. Ella let out—*accidentally*—a loud, gigantic TOOT.

Embarrassed, Ella snatched up the slipper and quickly ran to her carriage.

Devastated, the prince watched his true love's carriage drive off into the distance. The girl he wanted to marry was gone. The only thing that remained of her was a distinct smell that lingered. It was the fading scent of the girl's monstrous toot. The prince breathed deep.

He could not quite tell what it smelled like, but he knew he would never forget it.

The prince paced the steps, desperate for an idea—a way to find the girl. Suddenly, he knew. Racing to the palace kitchen, he collected ingredient after ingredient...

Beef. Broccoli. Cabbage. Falafel. Fresh-picked cherries. Yogurt. Apples. Brussels sprouts. And beans, lots of beans. Navy beans, garbanzo beans, black beans, brown beans, pinto beans, white beans.

The prince threw everything into the biggest pot he could find. He was stirring it all together when his father came into the kitchen for breakfast.

"My boy, what *are* you cooking?" the king asked.
"You can't *possibly* plan to eat that. Why, it would make you toot immediately!"

"Exactly," said the prince. "I plan to give this to each maiden in the kingdom to make them toot. The smell of their toots will lead me to my *true love*."

That very day, the king sent out his messenger with a royal proclamation: each maiden in the land was to drink the prince's potion and toot. Break wind. Cut the cheese. You know—fart. The prince and his guard would travel throughout the kingdom, smelling each maiden's toot. They would be on a mission to find the girl who had captured the prince's heart—

as well as his nose.

At the news of the mystery girl and the prince's quest, the kingdom
came alive. Maidens all over gasped in horror at the thought
of tooting on purpose—and in front of the prince! But each
knew that if a fart could win the prince's love,

it would be worth it.

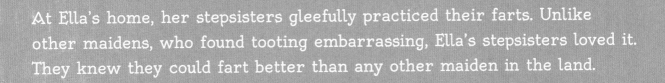

At Ella's home, her stepsisters gleefully practiced their farts. Unlike other maidens, who found tooting embarrassing, Ella's stepsisters loved it. They knew they could fart better than any other maiden in the land.

"Do you think the prince will like it?" the younger sister, Tootsie, asked.

"Definitely not," said Windy, the older sister. "How about this one?"

"If only we knew the smell of the toot that captured the prince's heart. What *could* it be?" they wondered aloud.

Ella tried not to listen as she cleaned the floors.

"Don't worry, Cinder-Ella," Windy said. "Keep cleaning. Maybe if you clean well enough, you can become Cinder-Toot!"

The girls laughed, and then ran away to continue practicing their... you know.

Ella nearly cried. She could only hope that the prince would recognize her—
and her smell.

The next day, the prince and his guard set out. House by house, they offered the prince's secret, wondrous concoction to each maiden they met.

ROTTEN EGG

SMELLY LITTER BOX

STINK BUG

ARMADILLO ARMPIT

It was no use. No matter how many homes the prince visited, no toot matched the smell of his true love. By the time the prince reached Ella's house, he was starting to believe that the woman of his dreams *wasn't even real*.

Inside the house, Ella's stepsisters and stepmother watched as the prince's carriage arrived. Grabbing Ella by the arm, her stepmother dragged her to the attic—and locked her in. She didn't want the prince to know about Ella, and she *certainly* didn't want Ella to distract the prince while her daughters were farting.

Ella looked out the lone window and saw the prince walking up to her very own front door. She couldn't believe she might miss her chance at seeing him again.

Her heart felt as if it were about to break.

Below her, the prince and his guard entered the house. Ella's stepmother and stepsisters stood eagerly, ready to win a prince. "Well, you know the deal," said the guard. "Let's have it. One at a time, please. Take a sip." The guard had clearly done this before, and wanted this *long*, *stinky quest* for the perfect toot to end.

The older sister tooted first. It smelled like . . .

"*Rotten fish!*" the prince groaned and held his nose.
"No! That is clearly not the smell I remember."

Next, the younger sister took a big swallow of the prince's potion.

"*Pirate breath!*" cried the prince, nearing tears.
"Definitely not it."

In the attic, Ella heard the thundering sounds of the toots below.
She wished she could reach her prince,
but she was helpless.

Suddenly, Ella had an idea. Mustering every ounce
of gas in her whole body, she jumped up and down,
bent this way and that, twisted her body as much
as she could, and . . .

...tooted.
Farted.
Over and over.
Again and again
and again.

Now she just had to hope that
the smell of her toot would seep
under the door, into the hallway, and
down the stairs to where the prince
and his guard stood—*before* they left!

Downstairs, the prince turned to his guard. "It seems my true love is nowhere to be found," he said gloomily. "I have smelled the toot of every maiden in the kingdom. *My true love is lost to me forever.*"

Defeated, the prince started to walk out the door. Then, suddenly, he stopped. The smell from Ella's toots had spread down the stairs, bursting through the house, door, and windows.

The prince sniffed.

What *was* that foul smell?

The prince sniffed again.

The aroma was unique, but familiar.
Something he had only smelled one time before.
"Is there anyone else in this house—another maiden,
perhaps?" the guard asked.
"No, no! Only my two beautiful daughters,"
Ella's stepmother replied.

Sniff! Sniff!

But the prince, mesmerized by the wondrous smell, was already starting to follow his nose. The smell led him up the stairs, through the hallway, and right to a locked door.

"This is it!" he said. "This is the smell I remember. This is the smell of my one true love!"

Without hesitation, the guard broke down the door, for unlike the prince, he couldn't handle another second in this stench.

In the middle of the room stood beautiful $Ella$, holding her precious slippers.

The prince stepped into the room and took a giant whiff.

"It's you!" he said.

Ella nodded, tears streaming down her cheeks. *"You found me!"*

The prince and Ella were married the very next day.

As Ella said "I do," a tear slid down her face.
And then she tooted—accidentally, of course.

The prince grinned.

*Fairy tales do come true,
after all.*

About the Author

John grew up with a love of falafel, beans, and great stories—thus he was destined to write a fairy tale about toots. While his daytime disguise is being an attorney, by night John and his kids dream up tales of joy and sometimes, well, flatulence. John lives in Michigan with his superhero wife, four kids, and a dog. You can learn more about John, plus a few surprises, at www.JohnMashni.com.

About the Illustrator

Kate Cosgrove is an award winning kidlit illustrator and artist. Her picture book *And The Bullfrogs Sing: A Life Cycle Begins*, published by Holiday House, debuted in 2019. Cosgrove's next book *The Dirt Book: Poems About Animals that Live Beneath Our Feet* is slated for release in June 2021. She writes and illustrates Junicorn, a weekly web comic, with her 10 year-old daughter. Kate's dog "Stinky" Stanley, the gassiest dog in the land, provided an authentic smellscape for her while she illustrated this book.

A Word from the Author

If you enjoyed this book, we would appreciate if you could take a minute to leave a review wherever you purchased the book, as your feedback helps others find this book. It also gives me (the author) encouragement to write more books based on the stories that I have told my children. Best of all, it helps other adults discover this story so they can share it with the children in their lives.

For fun and some free stuff, check out www.CinderToot.com.

Interested in buying bulk copies? I'll send you something hilarious if you do.

Go to www.CinderToot.com for more info.

A percentage of the profits from the sale of this book will go to a charity that serves those in need in our local community.

Mark 10:15

Made in the USA
Monee, IL
22 June 2021